HOI

A collection of sto

by members of

The Write Network 2013

Edited by Paula David

First published by The Write Network 2013.

Poems and stories copyright © individual authors 2013.

Artwork copyright© individual artists 2013.

Cover design by Myrto Williams.

Chief editor Paula David.

Copy editor Ruth Goldsmith.

Printed by Russell Press Ltd
Russell House, Bulwell Lane,
Nottinghamshire,
NG6 0BT, United Kingdom.

ISBN: 978-0-9926299-0-8

CONTENTS

An introductory note about the publisher

The Write Network was launched in January 2013 with the support of the charity Unlimited. Its mission is to support new writers by giving them the opportunity, confidence and skills to perform and publish their work. The Write Network exists to encourage those who may be less visible in the world of literature, such as ethnic minority groups and new but mature writers. The Write Network works for the unheard voices and makes the invisible visible.

Home is the first of The Write Network's annual anthologies!

For more information, see The Write Network website:

http://writenetwork.wordpress.com/about/

Foreword

Waltham Forest is the home of diversity. For generations, different cultures have existed side by side, sharing music, art, literature, exotic foods, fashions and different perspectives. The old and the new stand comfortably side by side, each respecting the other.

Twelve writers and two visual artists from Waltham Forest have interpreted the theme of *Home* for this anthology. Their contributions will give you reason to pause and think about the meaning of *Home*.

Paula David was born in London, UK. After completing a BA in Media and Creative Writing in 2007 at Middlesex University, London, she completed her first novel. It was longlisted in the Virginia Prize for unpublished novels (2009).

Paula has had stories and poems published in several anthologies. She has performed her own brand of performance poetry, which includes song and verse, all over London and beyond, including venues such as the Bishopsgate Institute, the Poetry Cafe, and the London Poetry Festival.

Paula's first play, *Second Chance*, won third prize in Newham's Playwright of the Year competition in 2009. Since then, her plays *Malachi, Helen's Help*, and *Second Chance* have had readings at Brockley Jack Theatre (June 2010), Stratford Circus (July 2010) and Jacksons Lane Theatre (May 2010). Her first full production, *Stories of Migration*, produced in May 2013, was performed to a sold out audience at Leyton Library.

Paula was Resident Artist at Stratford Circus in 2010, Writer in Residence for Rowan Arts in April 2011 and Writer in Residence at Leytonstone Festival in Summer 2012. She was awarded an MA in Creative and Professional Writing from Brunel University in September 2011.

Paula is the founder of The Write Network.

Finding my way back

I watched Stuart from across the breakfast table, hunched over his cereal bowl as if he was protecting it from predators. His hair had grown long and he was unshaven. When he rose to put his blazer on, I felt the urge to stop him, to make him stay. He gently kissed me on my forehead. I looked up at him. I could feel the empty, cold space between us. I wanted to name the void, my lips parted.

'I'll be home before you know it,' he said quickly.

I pressed my lips together and held onto the name.

'Go out and get some air, take Ellie to the park.'

I looked at Ellie happily picking at her dry coco pops. She was so quiet, almost absent. I turned back to Stuart to agree with his suggestion. Instead I watched the kitchen door click shut. I took a deep breath and rose to gather the things needed for a trip to the park.

I pushed the pram slowly, watching the gold and red leaves drift to the ground in a shower of autumn colours. My eyes closed and my feet stopped without effort. My mind and body were acting without consultation, again. Susie was wearing her red and beige polka dot woollen coat, trying to crush every leaf that presented itself to her. The scent of wet earth hung in the air. I breathed deeply, allowing the memory to prick my eyes and drain away.

Ellie was still asleep in the double buggy; the sight of the empty seat next to her tugged at my stomach. Trying desperately not to allow Susie's face to become visible to me again I grabbed the blue blanket, from Ellie's lap, and spread it over the empty seat.

A little breathless I collapsed onto a damp bench, with the pram facing the other way. Ellie stirred. A gentle high pitched moan accompanied the sound of her shoe falling to the ground. They were Susie's shoes. I had dressed Ellie in Susie's green patent shoes. Within moments, I was staring at Susie, next to the pram, in the green shoes. Her eyes were red and swollen, her faced crumpled in distress mouthing the word mummy, over and over. I felt desperate to hear her voice. Her clenched fists pounded the car window and the flames rose around her, still no sound. 'I'm sorry, I'm sorry,' I repeated louder and louder until I was screaming. Sweat tricked down my face. I didn't get to her in time. I couldn't get to her in time. I heard her voice calling me. I held my breath and lunged forward. She was in my arms, her cheek against mine, her little arms around my neck.

'Susie!'

I held her away from me to check that she was OK and realised I was holding Ellie. Disappointment rushed through me. I sat Ellie in the pram and stared at her.

'What's wrong, mummy?' said Ellie.

Her voice was always slightly lower than Susie's, but somehow today it was sweeter, almost tangible, so real. I felt as if I was hearing it for the first time.

I took her in my arms. She was warm and soft and still here.

Home

Home emerges in the first moment

as lips touch and love begins

to spring from an expectant soul.

Home the first gaze locked

and sealed for just a fraction of time

but will seem endless in memory.

Home is the harmony

that sweeps around two bodies

that know what is about to take place.

Home is the highest, sweetest,

rise of spirits sealed in momentary love,

and purr, in the aftermath.

Home is in the kiss goodbye

that promises days, weeks,

months and years of a union that will create life.

Roger Huddle continues to live in Walthamstow where he was born a very long time ago. He began writing after a serious illness led him to reassess his life in 2001. Taking severance from work, and apart being a volunteer at the William Morris Gallery, he is now officially retired. He studied creative writing at Birkbeck before doing a MA in Writing the Visual at the Norwich School of Art and Design with poet George Szirtes in 2007. In his working life, he was a graphic designer and photographer. He is writing a history of the socialist movement in Walthamstow and a fragmented memoir.

The great domed line of the sky: part one

T he earth was sodden. I followed two dog walkers and their dogs into the forest, along an often-used path cutting through thick grass made tall by a wet spring. At the edge of the trees walkers and dogs forked left, I went right and started to climb up the sunken and covered reservoir.

This mammoth piece of earth-moving and engineering was started in 1967 and finished in 1970. Now a clearing in the forest, nature has disguised the surface, the grass-covered mound resembles a Stone Age burial ground. This is the fourth water storage facility at Waterworks Corner and its height altered the landscape of my childhood. Holding twenty-seven million gallons, it sends feeders out to Woodford, Buckhurst Hill and as far as Loughton. A footbridge runs from the top of the mound across Forest Road, becoming a path through the forest towards Whipps Cross. Three smaller covered tanks and the pumping station can be seen from the footbridge; these are not covered with nature, but brick, iron and concrete.

The waterworks were started in 1876 on part of Epping Forest bought from the Crown and on land purchased, after much wheeling and dealing, from local landowner Henry Maynard, by the ruthless East London Water Company. The buildings, as with all those built by the water board, took architectural inspiration from a classical Italian style, in brick rather than stone. The pumping station brings water up from the Lea Valley and is at the top of one of the tallest hills in the town, marking the border with Woodford. Waterworks Corner is where you enter or leave.

I was early, the light barely arriving against a slow-moving leaden sky, white to dark clouds floating to the horizon and beyond. I stopped in the centre of the bridge, to watch a woman on the road below jog towards me. I kept watching until she passed below; panting, carrying her iPlayer, attached to her ears with white cord. I cannot understand why runners prefer running to music, watching the ground, enclosed, instead of watching the light shift, sounds change, sometimes a deafening silence – a continuous collection of moments.

I looked down across the Lea Valley thinking of how William Morris had seen '...the wide green sea of the Essex marshland, with the great domed line of the sky and the sun shining down in one peaceful light over the great distance'. Houses and factories now block the view, but I still find it breathtaking looking towards the hills of Waterlow Park, Highgate, and Hampstead on the far horizon. Over Muswell Hill, the 'People's Palace' catches a ray of sunlight from a small break in the clouds to show off its newly washed yellow London brickwork. From this spot, with a telescope, in the early nineteenth century, on a Sunday morning, I might have watched John Keats make his way down from the Heath, across the river at the Ferry Boat Inn, and up Marsh Street, now the High Street, to have lunch with his sister Fanny in the big house of her guardian Richard Abbey. He was an all-round pillar of local society, who thought that poetry was a ruinous and misguided occupation: he was antagonistic to the poet's work and bohemian influence, going as far in October 1818 as forbidding Fanny to see him. It was only Keats's love of his young sister and sadness for her lonely enslavement in the Abbey household that brought him across that wide green sea.

Off the bridge I followed the fence bordering the Waterworks, looking for a path that would take me down to the road. Far away to my left, above the trees were the distinctive silhouettes, including the 'Gherkin', of the City in the twenty-first century, and over my shoulder barely visible, the rival camp for finance capital at Canary Wharf. From this point I can only feel the sprawl of East London lying before me: it is hidden beyond the forest with the Thames its far boundary. I turned down a slippery path, avoiding brambles and a white rose bush that had escaped a garden to become wild and free on the edge of the woods. I slipped out onto Forest Road.

I set off downhill, with a plan to walk straight across the borough to Tottenham. The morning rush hour is building, not bad because it's still half term: no kids, parents, no teachers. There is local traffic, plus vehicles coming from East Anglia and Cambridgeshire off the M11, maybe some arriving from the Thames estuary urban sprawl via the A13. Many central London bound drivers go further around before turning into the centre, staying on the A406 or turning further out onto the orbital, dropping off at the A12, Enfield,

Potters Bar, South Mimms or Hendon, or in the opposite direction across the Queen Elizabeth to the Medway Towns, Gatwick, Royal Tunbridge Wells, Hastings. There is enough to fill the air with exhaust and noise: delivery vans, single occupant cars, drivers in a race to get to their desk quicker than anyone else or desperate to make up time at the start of the day so as to be able to work later, lengthening the work day to shorten their working life. Always the huge juggernauts cutting across to enter the City at Finsbury Park, Camden or down the Caledonian Road to Kings Cross, and not forgetting the age old 123 bus that has run from Ilford to Turnpike Lane for as long as I can remember. The AEC Routemaster taken weekly during my adolescent years: Tuesdays to the Ilford Palais Mecca Dance Hall, and on Thursday and Saturdays to the Tottenham Royal Mecca Dance Hall. I could really dance, we were modernists: pork pie hats and mohair suits, Ben Sherman button down shirts, Ravel brogues and made to measure hipsters from Nino's in West Green Road, hair cut in Green Lanes at Manor House, always on the move away from home, in pairs, in gangs. Watching the opening sequence of Martin Scorsese's Mean Streets in 1973, I had the disturbing feeling that we had been trying hard to look like a bunch of Eastside New York mafia trainees – wise guys.

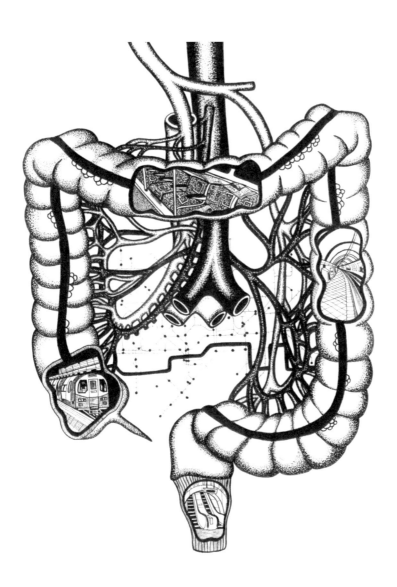

Ruth Goldsmith was born in 1980. She has spent much of her spare time since then dreaming of the day when a novel would be published with her name on the spine.

Four years of studying the classics of English and French Literature at university crushed any such pretensions for a decade. In search of rehabilitation, Ruth began attending creative writing classes. Still in recovery, she has thankfully reached a point where she can now just get on with writing for pleasure.

Ruth enjoys writing short stories, as a way of capturing the world around her or escaping from it completely. She is working on her first novel, inspired by an encounter with a portrait from late 16th-century Italy and her desire to tell the story of the strange young woman it depicts.

When not on maternity leave, Ruth is Communications Manager for a drug policy charity. She lives near Walthamstow Marshes with Tom, their baby daughter, Bea, a small black cat called Zodiac and hundreds of books.

Giganticus

It appeared one day between the second-to-last and last floorboards in the hall, right up against the door lintel. A tiny green tendril, curling round upon itself. It looked like a piece of horticultural litter, a stowaway on my shoe. But when I tried to brush it between the floorboards with my toe, it didn't budge.

I bent down and tugged. There was a weight to whatever it was, growing there, underneath my floor. I didn't give the matter much thought. Already late, I shut the door behind me and hurried to catch my train.

By the time I turned the key in the lock that evening, the tendril had doubled in length. I carefully stepped over it and flicked on the light, took off my jacket and got down on my hands and knees, until I could smell the wood varnish. I peered at it.

The tendril now sported a single leaf. The leaf looked like those on the parsley I bought in improbably large bunches from the International Supermarket. It didn't smell like parsley though. Minuscule downy hairs grew from the stem. Bent over in the hallway, I could see no other identifying features. I pinched it between my thumb and forefinger and pulled, until I felt something snap. I could see nothing more between the floorboards.

I placed the specimen on the kitchen side, next to the toaster. I'd no idea what sort of weed could be growing up through my floor; I wasn't at all green fingered. I just wanted rid of it before it caused any bother.

The following morning, it came as something of a shock that the kitchen worktop was no longer visible. The mass of vegetation exuded a faint, cabbage-like scent. Flat, angular leaves the size of my outstretched hand unfurled on the hob. Thick green stems entwined themselves around my mug tree. Pale white roots dripped down the cupboard doors towards the floor.

And then I went into the hall.

It took three goes with the saw to hack my way through the thick, woody stem that had forced its way out of the skirting board, scattering pine splinters and crumbs of plaster. The plant was up to my waist. I threw the saw back through the door once I'd managed to get out. I missed my train.

During my lunchbreak, I rang the Council and asked them to send someone urgently. After some discussion over the definition of 'urgent', I was told a Customer Services Representative from Environment and Refuse Services would be round in a few days.

When Bob finally arrived in his Council-branded van, the whole downstairs of the house was alive. I'd given up using the front door by then. The plant was growing up my bookshelves, curling round the dining table, up between floorboards, anywhere it could get a foothold. It had also started to flower – beautiful, delicate white stars, exploding constellations at the end of each stalk.

Bob stood in the front garden, next to the wheelie bins, and looked in through the living room window. His mouth and eyes were wide open. They stayed that way for ages. I invited him to clamber in, but he said he was all right, thanks. He took some photos, wrote in his notebook and went to sit in his van to make phone calls. I couldn't hear what he said.

After Bob's visit, things moved quickly. Three more members of the Council's Environment and Refuse Services dropped in. Then a man from the Department for Environment, Food and Rural Affairs, or Defra, came, accompanied by others in protective clothing. They took away samples of my plant, and lifted up the floor in the hall. By that time, I'd started watering it. I'd had to move most of my stuff upstairs anyway, and until they knew what it was, it seemed cruel not to. The man from Defra looked at me a bit strangely when I said that.

As it turned out, my plant wasn't a weed after all. It was something special: an extremely rare species called creeping marshwort, Latin name *Apium repens*. Creeping marshwort, I was told, at a meeting in Whitehall with a civil servant from Defra, is only found in three places in the UK, including Walthamstow Marshes. The civil servant explained that it had crept its way into my house from the Marsh through some long abandoned piping related to the Coppermill Lane reservoirs. There, it seems, it had encountered some chemical residues used in the water treatment process. Defra scientists believed these chemicals had caused the marshwort to grow to at least fifteen times its normal size. The water company, sensing a law suit, were refuting this.

The man in the grey suit across the table in Whitehall said that the plant was highly protected under UK and EU law. He said he was sorry, but that it couldn't be removed, even if it had taken over the downstairs of my house. The fact that my plant was a supersized specimen, never before seen by the international scientific community, only enhanced its protected status.

Once the plant pushed up floorboards and sprouted through carpets in my neighbours' houses, the story got out. Camera crews arrived. As the first 'marshwort victim', I was in demand. Environmentalists and politicians debated 'the marshwort invasion' in news studios.

Three years on, all the houses on my old street have been reclaimed for the Marshes by the supersized creeping marshwort, or *Apium repens giganticus*, to give it its proper scientific name. The street's now a nature reserve, with a visitor centre and research laboratory. Scientists come from all over the world. Estate agents talk about the 'marshwort boom' in the Walthamstow rental market.

I'm pleased the plant chose me. Of course, it was hard to begin with, moving into temporary accommodation while things got sorted in the courts. But now the compensation is through, life is good. I stroll past my old home most days, on the way to my allotment, where I've discovered I have a real talent for growing things. The house has almost completely disappeared into green, bricks and mortar crumbling under the force of new growth.

Trevor David is 45 years old. He was born in Sheffield, England, to Jamaican parents from mixed heritages. He has lived in various places, including Wales, Jamaica and Germany and chose to settle down in Walthamstow 12 years ago.

He began writing about the adventures of fantastical figures around the age of nine. His imagination and writing proved to be a haven from the world around him. He went on to take pleasure in writing poems. Two childhood memories, which he values greatly, are his introduction to *Rats* by James Herbert and when a poem he submitted to *The Voice* (a black British newspaper) was published.

He extended his love of writing to drama and music. In his twenties, he worked as a singer/songwriter with various bands and producers. He went on to publish articles for medical and psychological journals and appeared in the *Identities Unite* anthology. As a self-confessed geek, he especially enjoys the genres of science fiction and fantasy. He believes fantasy-based fiction provides the opportunity to discover what 'normal' people do under 'abnormal' circumstances.

His short-term ambition is to continue to write and perform his material. Eventually he would like publish fantasy-based works of fiction.

Homecoming

'I go down to your water and I won't turn away …' Silky jazz drifts through the car stereo

"Turn that radio off, it's upsetting Nick."

Dr Peters responds "Nurse Julie, I could play death metal and the boy would not flinch."

"Don't worry Nick, we'll be there soon."

Julie's voice is too soft to get through the din in Nick's head. His taut body continues to rock back and forth. His arms are clenched and folded into a misshapen cross. She slides closer to him, avoids the embrace she longs to offer. Her heart remains heavy with the desire to soothe and caress. Instead she places her marshmallow fingers on his lap. He continues to rock, oblivious to the intrusion. Without thought she taps, no reaction. She attempts to catch his eye and shows a wide smile, nothing.

Three figures stand outside Nick's destination. Each one has been to see him during his stay in hospital. Each had found it difficult to see his condition. All each could do was watch as this wounded animal switched between docile and feral, moment to moment. Physical contact was not permitted. Maris had perhaps found this the hardest, but had not expressed it to anyone.

In preparation for his return, she spent the week cleaning. There was not a fleck of dust or smear of grime left. She had even got Stevie to sort out his pit of a bedroom. The foul smell that started in his room and snaked around the rest of the house was gone. She had not needed to use air fresheners for two days now. Oh what is to have a thirteen year old son. A boy who has grown to tower over you and in fact was now taller than his father. Yet he remained a child, selfish and unruly, just like his father.

Where she was the one who held them together, the one who remained positive and the one who organised the posters, the interviews. The one who prevented the details of what that man did to her son reaching the public. It was she who made sure they were waiting, in their Sunday best, for Nick's homecoming. They had been standing by the gate for an hour. She would not let either Stevie or his dad move. Bubbles may have been rising in her stomach, her bladder may have been full, but they would remain there until Nick came home and now he was.

The car parks in front of the three waiting figures, Maris rushes to the car to hold her seventeen-year-old first born. She opens the back seat door.

"Nick you're home."

This is not the vision Nick had imagined. He opens his mouth wide to mouth the words, "This isn't home, liars, liars, liars."

Instead are screams from his gut, growls of disbelief and rage.

"Nick baby, it's us your family."

Dr Peters interrupts, "No Mrs Matthews, allow him to settle first."

"But you said he was better... Ready to come home, but look at him he's..."

"Mrs Matthews, I said it would take time."

"Time, it's been..."

"That returning to a familiar environment might..."

Nick jerks his body back over the lap of Nurse Julie. He hits his head on the door handle opposite. Over and over he thumps his head backwards, with each contact the thuds become louder. Nurse Julie attempts to restrain him. He slows slightly, when cool liquid oozes from the splits in his scalp. The injuries become memories of his lover's touch, they flood his senses until all he feels is numbness.

He opens his eyes, only to see strangers. He screams from the back of throat, "Home."

All movement stops, the commotion of grappling, grabbing stops, bird song and insect buzz stop. His bellow is rebounded by screeching silence. All stare, Dr Peters, Nurse Julie, mother, father and brother. They all stop. Stop and stare at Nick.

Joy rushes through Maris. The delicate figure crouching in a ball is no longer silent.

"He spoke, my Nicky spoke. Yes darling, this is your home."

Nick had formed a word. The strength of a simple syllable grated the back of his throat. A foreign familiar muscle had started and was not ready to stop.

"No... Not home... Home ... Home... Want my home."

Maris' joy does not last long confronted with his words. This is not her son, his voice, his spirit. She looks at this strange, dishevelled figure and sees nothing of the child that was taken from her, only the remains of what was done to him. What is he now?

The fake strength that held Maris over the last eleven years drains from her muscles; her stoic stance reveals fragility. As her limbs loosen, thick jelly tears gather at her lower eyelids. Drip down her face and settle on the part grimace, part smile of her mouth.

She pushes past Dr Peters, pours into the backseat of the car and seizes Nick. She easily pulls his emaciated frame out towards her. Her 5ft 7" frame towers over him. Her body gives an involuntary shiver and recoils slightly. This is the first time she has held him since his abduction and all she feels are bones.

Nick fights against her hold, but he is no match for her strength. As he attempts to slide down her arms, she squeezes him closer. On his back, old torture wounds that had begun to heal begin to weep. Echoes of his captor's touch return to Nick's mind, his body becomes rubber, in preparation for the pain that usually followed.

Maris swallows; she pushes down her anger, revulsion, despair and clings on to her hope. She straightens her spine, looks directly into Nick's eyes and says, "Now listen to me, this is your home and you will be staying here with your family. Do you understand? I don't care if you bite, scratch or kick me. It won't change a thing. You're home and that is it."

Nick looks into her eyes and then at the strangers around him. He wonders if home is where the heart is, and his heart has been torn from him, will he ever be home again.

Father and younger son look on motionless as Maris and Nick walk together towards the house.

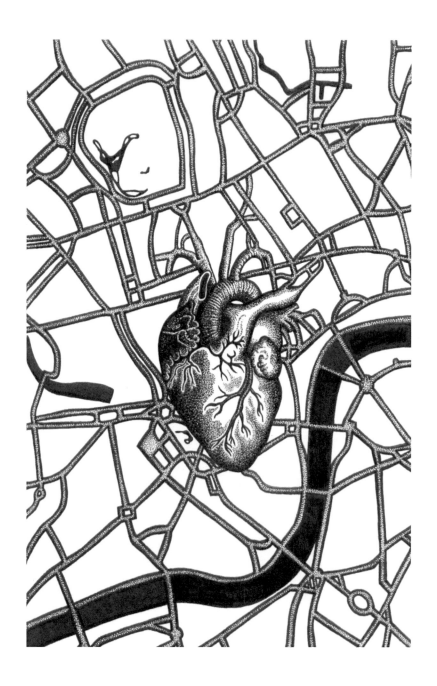

Marcia White has always enjoyed writing and has been crafting short stories on and off for around 20 years, and is currently experiencing regeneration in thought and word. Her interest in "great" literature was sparked at high school and the bold works of authors such as Chinua Achebe, James Baldwin and F. Scott Fitzgerald, who offered an alternative perspective of the world.

As a black British woman of Caribbean descent, she includes Toni Morrison, Maya Angelou and Alice Walker amongst the growing list of incredible black women writers on her bookshelf, who provide a constant source of creative inspiration, through their strong cultural identity, poetic and authentic voices of the unheard.

Marcia was fortunate to have spent her formative years in between England and the Caribbean where her passion for writing was fed by the poetry of the spoken word and the creative use of language – as a conveyor of culture, tool of social commentary and repository of oral archive.

She has always written for personal pleasure and delights in the responses that her short stories evoke. Marcia lives in Waltham Forest and has two children.

Home

"You've made this place look really nice." Dawn had entered without knocking. She always did.

"It's the best I can do for now," Sandra smiled. She'd had lots of practice in her brief 18 years. "This place will be a real home."

The wardrobe, wood polished and glistening white, would fit nicely here, alongside matching blinds. She'd seen them on *Neighbours*, her favourite soap.

Sandra's choices were very different from the rooms she'd decorated growing up. She always painted with care, muscles aching by the final brush stroke. Pleasure in a job well done was always short-lived as she awaited the next move.

Each move chipped away at the image of the ideal home Sandra carried in her head. She became skilled at juggling the bin bags of her possessions up narrow winding stairs, into lifts reeking of stale urine, across rubbish-strewn courtyards, well manicured lawns to new homes.

New homes where red-eyed youngsters bit furiously on lower lips to stem the hurt from spilling over. Homes where bright smiles hid empty emotions and robotic repetition. Homes which were stop gaps to the next home.

Dawn reminded Sandra of Mum, who always enthused over every brush stroke and the 'best home ever'. Ever optimistic, Mum would say, "Guess what? We've got a new home – it'll be the best home ever!" Sandra could smell bread baking in the oven as Mum talked of cosy evenings watching TV on the sofa. With every move, every "Guess what?" Mum's voice ascended an octave, her bright lipstick framed by the neat red haired bob.

Mum never said "new flat" or "new bedsit", it was always "we've got a new home". But Mum had never moved from the leafy semi she'd bought in the 1980s – next door to the village school. Sandra had never visited the house, she'd not seen the kids in the playground nor the attentive teachers.

Mrs Matthews was the only teacher Sandra could remember – Year 5. Her third teacher that year. Her third new home, third school, third school uniform donated from the charity box. The third bus route she memorised because she'd never been at any school long enough to learn how to read or write properly. Sandra recalled when she took the wrong bus back home. Her absence sparked a police search. An officer found her 15 miles from where she should've been, crouched in a corner of the bus depot, cold, hungry and crying. She was 11. Sandra was called 'silly' and 'selfish' and told off for running away. Only Mum believed she'd forgotten the way back.

Sandra missed Mum and their long talks. Mum was the only one who cared. "You need to go out more, make some friends," Mum would say, opening the curtains in Sandra's room for the first time in days. "People like you," she'd add, before recounting stories of her family.

But even Mum was too late to save Sandra's locket, given to her by a grandmother she had never met. It was with the fading photo of baby Sandra with Mum and Dad, and her drawing of a house with a tree and yellow sun, which Mrs Matthews had adorned with stars and the words "Well done Sandra!" in neat bright red letters. Mistaken for rubbish at the home she'd arrived the night before, with her life in black bin bags, it was the drawing and locket which Sandra remembered most.

Mum cried more than Sandra at their loss. At her funeral, Sandra discovered Mum had dozens of children. Like Sandra, some had known Mum for years. Sandra was the only one who called her "Mum". By then Sandra had a new Mum, but she was just a social worker to Sandra.

It was days later that Sandra, still grieving, decided to follow Mum's advice to get out more. "You can do better than this lot," Mum would've said of her new friends – alcoholics, thieves, addicts – even though they were the very people Mum lived for. People who society forgot and respectable neighbours kept wary tabs on through twitching net curtains. Sandra visited her friends often, stepping carefully through overgrown gardens, clambering through broken windows to meet in dingy little rooms. She, hungry for the highs that made her life tolerable, them, eager for the companionship she offered. It was accepted that one day they may just not be there. Transitory chaos was the norm.

But now Sandra's new home was streets away from that life. Clean and orderly, she knew all her neighbours. The rules of "community" were simple – when to be friendly, when to keep distance. They had all made a choice to be there. Many had settled years before and weren't looking to move on. "I'm happy here – or as happy as I've ever been in any home,"

Kate next door told her.

A patch of weak sun on the wall above her bed, often teased her to come outside. Today it was strong and bright. Sandra could feel its warmth coating the room even though she was not in its direct path. Looking to the single window, branded by the now familiar vertical pattern, Sandra glimpsed Dawn staring at the watercolour of the sunset hanging opposite. "Did you paint these?"

Sandra nodded, sweeping her arm around the room to display the market scene and the fishing harbour, brought alive with rich and vivid colours. She longed to enjoy the sun outside. But that decision was not hers to make, neither the choice to visit her neighbours, go on the landing or choose what to eat and when. The rules of her home were dictated by those who held the keys to her life for the next eight years and nine months. "Out in five and half if you're good," Dawn said. "You've got the rest of your life ahead of you after that – lesson learned."

Sandra didn't know if she wanted to be "good". She liked her home and the certainty it offered, no false promises of baking bread and cosy evenings. She was settled, she wanted to stay forever.

Dawn smiled as she backed out the room, pulling closed the door. The key turned with a loud clunk.

Sandra looked around the 12 by 10ft room and said aloud: "Guess what Mum? This is my best home ever."

Walthamstow-based writer **Esther Freeman** has been writing short stories since she was in primary school. These stories generally involved her cat who developed a number of human-like abilities and characteristics. Sadly these stories have never been published.

Since then Esther has focused on storytelling through documentary film making. She has also worked as a ghost writer for a number of leading non-profit organisations, with articles published in *The Guardian* and *Independent.*

Deciding she'd like to finally have a bit of glory for herself she embarked on a creative writing course at Central St Martin's College in 2010. It was here the idea for her first completed novel, *Burning Ants,* was born.

Esther is currently working on her second novel, which is based on the real life stories of unsung female heroes during World War Two. She's also a part time blogger, writing about fashion and feminism.

Dan the man

It's my birthday today. I've got a cake. It's blue and it's got my name on. Danny, it says. The cake has candles - 18 of them. 1234567891011121314151617 18. I like counting candles. Mum says candles aren't for counting, they're for blowing out. I prefer counting them.

Nanna and Grandad came over. Granddad got me a book about birds with a CD of their songs. Granddad thought I was clever because I knew which song went with which bird.

Mum gave me a present. The wrapping paper was red and shiny and it felt nice when I ripped it open.

"It's an X-box," she said.

"Oh."

Granddad folded his arms, which meant he was angry. "Say thank you, son."

He calls me 'son', but he's not my Dad. My Dad lives with the Dirty Slapper From Skegness.

Mum had her upside down face on. "What's wrong? Don't you like it?"

"I wanted something else."

"What?"

"A girlfriend."

They all looked at me with upside down faces. It made me confused and scared.

Then Nanna started laughing, which made her big belly jiggle about. "I don't think you can buy one of those in the corner shop," she said.

Granddad was laughing too. "And if you do, you should definitely keep the receipt."

Now all three of them were laughing.

I hated it when they did this.

"You don't find them in a shop," I shouted. "You find them in parks and pubs. Now I'm 18 I can have a girlfriend. Mum can get me one."

Mum did a sigh. "Well, I don't know ... "

"But you're good at finding things, Mum. You always find Nanna's glasses when she loses them."

"It's not quite the same, love."

"It is!"

"Danny, calm down."

"But I want a girlfriend so I can stick my thingy in her."

Nanna did an O shape with her mouth.

Granddad jumped up and had a really red face. "Enough!" he yelled.

"It's not fair," I said, but really quietly.

I kept thinking about the girlfriend. I would even dream of her and when I woke up my thingy would be all big and I'd feel strange.

One time Mum saw and said: "Where's my baby boy gone?"

I thought this was a silly thing to say because I was right in front of her.

At the Day Centre, Mrs Baker told Mum I'd been looking down Mary Munroe's knickers. Mum didn't say anything the whole way home. When we got to the house she folded her arms, which meant she was cross. "You can't do things like that," she said.

"I said please."

"It doesn't matter."

"Why?"

"Sex is a special thing, between two people who… " Mum put her hand on her forehead. "Danny, do you understand what sex is?"

"When two people love each, then they kiss, then they go to the bedroom and – "

"Yes, ok."

"But me and Mary weren't having sex. I just – "

"You can't do that either."

"Why?"

"Enough questions. Go wash your hands, tea will be ready soon."

Me and Mum didn't talk about sex after that, which made me sad because I had lots of questions. Then one day she said we were going to London.

"Are we going to see Dad and the Dirty Slapper From Skegness?" I asked.

"No, we're not.

"So why are we going to London?"

"To find you a girlfriend. But it will only be for the day, ok?"

"Ok."

"And then that'll be the end of it, ok?"

"Ok."

"No more talk about girlfriends, and no more looking down Mary Munroe's knickers."

I wasn't very happy about this, so I just shrugged.

We went on the train and then on the underground. I was very excited. "What's my girlfriend's name?" I asked Mum.

"I don't know yet."

"Where will we find her?"

"There's a special street."

"A special street for girlfriends?"

Mum nodded.

I was very excited about the special street.

When we got there it was a magical place. There were red lights in the windows, and pretty girls stood in doorways smiling at us. Mum picked the best one and we went inside.

The fat man with the shiny, bald head looked at me with an upside down face. He had pictures of naked women painted on his arms and a big bushy mustache. He pulled aside a curtain made of pink and blue beads, and pointed down a dark corridor. "Last door on the right," he grunted.

I looked at Mum because I don't know my left and right. She took a pen from her handbag and put a cross on my right hand.

I opened the door and saw a lady sitting on a windowsill. I couldn't see her face, but I knew she was pretty because she had blond hair. She was wearing her knickers and a bra, and had pointy shoes with big, spiky heels. They were red and shiny, like my birthday wrapping paper.

"No kissing and no funny business," she said, without turning round.

Her voice was loud and sharp, not soft and squidgy like Mum's. She stubbed a cigarette out and stared at me.

My girlfriend was pretty, but she was also a bit scary. I felt a bit like crying.

Then my girlfriend's head flopped on one side and her voice went sort of quiet. She said. "What's up love?"

I wiped my nose on the sleeve of my jumper like Nanna tells me not to. "Mum said you would be my girlfriend, because I'm 18 now. But only for today."

"Is this for real?"

I wasn't sure what she meant, but I nodded anyway.

My girlfriend put her hands on her hips. "So you really want to, you know…?"

I didn't know, so I didn't say anything.

"You want me to be your girlfriend?"

"Yes please."

My girlfriend sighed and took my hand. "What's your name sweetheart?"

"Danny."

"Ok Danny, is this your first…am I your first girlfriend?"

I nodded.

"Are you nervous?"

I nodded again.

"Well … don't be. My name is Hope. I'm going to show you a real good time."

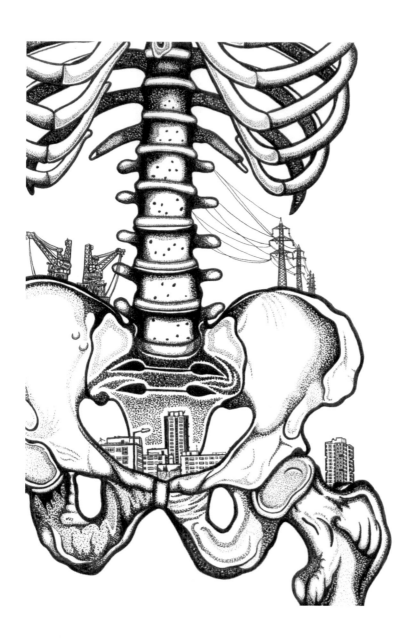

H. C. De Maria lives in Walthamstow. This is an excerpt from a longer work on the themes of home and homelessness in London.

Late

Late. Late awake. Late for work. Late out the door with the start of a hangover. Trying to run in her new work heels, falling and opening a raw scrape across her knee. Late to the station, Emily stands wheezing on the platform, swearing at her train as it shrinks into the distance.

Late into Victoria, trying hopelessly to hurry through the rush hour crush. Crowds close up around her, wall off every escape route, force her into step with everyone else. No exceptions, no excuses. She shuffles out from the station and seethes slowly up Victoria Street.

Images of work roll through her mind. The meeting she should be in. I should be taking the minutes. The Board. The Boardroom. Walking the length of it to get to her seat. Everyone looking. Why is this happening to me?

Emily is late and hot and angry and then baffled when the crowds part and she pushes into a striped plastic tape stretched across the pavement. She pauses, looks ahead up the road. A hundred yards from her building. Less. She shakes her head, swears and ducks under the tape.

A hand on her back as it rises, a voice of authority.

'Back behind the line please, there's been an incident.' A policewoman, bulky in vest, equipment, but shorter than Emily in her heels. Emily has learnt that you assert yourself if you want to get ahead. Fire or fall back.

'OK, no, look, I staff a Government Minister and I work like twenty yards the other side of that tape and I'm sodding late for work. So I'm going through. OK?'

The policewoman pauses for a moment, then points firmly back at the tape.

Emily stands her ground, stiffened by something in the ache behind her eyes, in the noise and the crowd, in the thought of what is happening at the office. She hesitates, then puts her head down and strides past the policewoman towards her office.

Emily makes four, five steps, and then a firm grip is bending her arm high up behind her, twisting, hurting. She shrieks, tries to wriggle free, fails, is overcome by panic. The grip doesn't move, doesn't shift. She subsides, holds still.

'Are you finished?' asks the policewoman.

Emily breathes deeply and tries to manage her rising fear. Tries to think. Brought up to respect law and order. Defer to authority. Be nice. Sod that, she thinks. Win or lose. She fetches up the voice she spent hours practising to impress in job interviews.

'Look, listen, you are making a big mistake. Let me go or I'll be making a formal complaint. Let me go right now.'

Nothing happens for a few long seconds. She is bent over, and all she sees are her shoes, the pavement, a cigarette butt.

Another hand lands firmly on her, gripping her shoulder and pulling her up to standing. Wordlessly, the policewoman gives Emily a firm shove to get her walking. Her shoes scrape on the pavement as she tries to keep from tripping, and she almost falls, the grip on her rigid, holding her up.

'Oi, that's a seriously expensive suit you are ruining,' she lies, 'and I will personally make sure you pay for it.'

Emily's voice still aims at imposing, but wavers and catches. Tears are starting in her eyes. The initial shock subsiding, her mind runs with fears. What's happening? Am I being arrested? Image of a prison cell. Her manager of three weeks having to bail her out. Her father having to bail her out. Stern faces, disappointment. Why is this happening to me?

Now that she's upright, she can see several of the milling crowd stopping and pointing their mobiles at her. She sees headlines, "Aide Embarrasses Minister – Forced To Resign". Why is this happening to me?

The policewoman steers her firmly to the other side of the pavement, to a gap between two shop fronts. A cubby hole, a few feet wide, half concealed by bins and black sacks of rubbish. Something in her brain sparks recognition of this spot, but she's confused, can't make the connection.

A man in what look like decorator's overalls is kneeling by the opening, and taking pictures of something behind the dustbins. Two other policemen stand by, talking. They all look bored.

The policewoman manoeuvres Emily to where she can see past the photographer. Her voice in Emily's ear is calm and quiet. She sounds tired.

'You're a big important person. OK. We're all getting in your way. Fair enough. Tell him that.'

Emily is not listening, twisting her head back, trying to catch the policewoman's eye, trying to apologise. She can't think straight, can't get the words out of her dry mouth. The policewoman holds her, silently, until she registers what is in front of her, and it is the smell that hits first. Acrid, burnt, she can taste it at the back of her throat.

In front of her a sleeping bag, old and dirty, is spread out in the little space behind the dustbins. Something is underneath it, person-sized, a foot in a tattered trainer protruding from one corner.

'Oh my God,' says Emily, 'what–'

'We don't think he was attacked here. Too busy and the shops have cameras. Looks like he crawled here after. Someone found him in the night and put the bag over him. Probably well gone by then. Maybe tried to give him a bit of dignity.'

Emily stares in bewilderment at the crumpled shape under the sleeping bag. Her point made, the policewoman's anger abates. She releases her grip, puts a softer hand on Emily's shoulder. She is making to steer Emily away when the photographer nods to one of the policemen, who reaches over and lifts away the sleeping bag.

The ground shifts sharply beneath Emily's feet, rolls and rises up to meet her. Then the policewoman is standing over her, telling her to breathe.

'I know him,' Emily manages to say, 'I know him.'

Eileen Bellot often describes her writing as a form of exorcism or an act of making sense of the world around her. Her written work is inspired by her curiosity of life, her artwork, dreams, self-exploration, fables and ritual. Eileen has written several articles through her work in arts education and running a health and wellbeing charity. Her poems and prose have been displayed through art exhibitions and more recently through podcast. She loves exploring storytelling to inspire creative thinking, self-development, teaching and as a means of empowering those she works with.

Eileen is currently working on a women's rites of passage project exploring the myths, fears and traditions around the menopause. The book will gather women's stories and experiences of the menopause to help demystify it and help women reclaim the menopause as the powerful rite of passage that it is.

Back home

I remember my maiden voyage to the land of my ancestors and of arriving in the centre of Roseau, the capital of Dominica, on a bright sunny Caribbean afternoon. I stood in the middle of the hustle and bustle, the toings and froings, lapping it all up. As if I was quenching a thirst of the sweetest deepest belonging. I felt a pride and ease that I couldn't quite comprehend and then at once it struck me; here was I in a sea of blackness, where I was no longer the minority but the majority. A resonance occurred; not only were all the people around me black, they were all Dominican. These were my people, not just my race, but my people. We were encoded with a DNA that fine-tuned us to a kindred frequency. Whilst that affinity vibrated my essence, an earthing took place right through to my core. This gave me a sense of belonging that I had never realised was lacking. I felt a sum of the greater part, a connection to the people, the land and all that had ever been before, in this place that we had fondly called Back Home.

Here I was in the place where so many of my mother's stories had their roots, the place where my mother, her mother and her mother before her had stood. I was struck by the lushness of the land and the expansiveness of untamed mountains that reached for the heavens. I had never imagined that green had so many hues. Each one made more luscious by the light of the sun that radiated their glow.

My sense of belonging received a rude awakening one day when I was walking through my mother's village, Scotts Head. One of the locals called out to me, "Hey English." I was in shock! English - I was being called English, hadn't they seen the colour of my skin, didn't they know I was Dominican too? Here was I in Dominica being called English by one of my own. During my six weeks in Dominica, I had to get used to being called English by the locals who didn't know my name. They could spot us a mile off before we had even opened our mouths. It wasn't our clothes that gave us away, it was the way we wore them, or the lack of ease in our bodies and maybe even our desire for forming orderly queues. Nobody queues for anything in Dominica!

As my holiday went on, I grew increasingly irked by people calling out, "Hey English." Then one day I blew my fuse and all my anger and frustration exploded onto this poor demure man, who thought he was just being friendly. I had to step back and reflect on why this was getting under my skin. If I was considered as foreign in England, the place of my birth and where I lived my life and foreign in Dominica, the place of my heritage and ancestry, then where was my home, where did I belong? This was a question that threw me and made me realise that I had to claim my own sense of home. I was a product of transition and lived in a country where I am in minority. I was raised with the ways of my mother and her people, but alas not their tongue, their features, but alas not their full reflection. I was raised in a land that gave my mother opportunity and her children things she never had. A union of the warm smooth Caribbean Sea and the choppy cold expansive Atlantic Ocean.

This was a trip of discovery on a level I had not fathomed; so where am I now? I have settled myself with the knowing that England is my home, the place I live and have built my life. Dominica is my soul's home, the place where my spirit and essence belongs. No matter how many times I am called 'English' in Dominica, it cannot shake from me the deep sense of belonging and affinity that I feel from the land. When I die I want to be cremated and my ashes taken in a container to the depths of the Caribbean Sea, at the tip of the island that is my mother's village. I want my ashes to be released, so that my bones can settle with the bones of my ancestors. In the place oddly enough, where the Caribbean Sea meets the Atlantic Ocean. I want to be taken Back Home, and who knows, maybe a few specks of my ashes might drift back along, the Atlantic Ocean.

Maja Dawson is originally from Derbyshire and went to the University of Leeds. Not long afterwards, she settled and worked in Reading for several years. Having spent six months volunteering and travelling in South America, she settled in London in 2009.

Maja has always enjoyed writing and often wrote poetry and kept diaries, but did not think about it seriously until a few years ago. She began by writing and illustrating children's fiction and would like to publish this someday.

This is an extract from a longer piece of work and is Maja's first attempt at a story for older readers. She worked for an academic year in a South London college, where many students were on the verge of gangs and crime. This story becomes a detective novel with many twists and turns. Maja believes passionately in the power of reading and would like to tell a story that young people could relate to.

Maja's Mum comes from Sweden and - although a little vague and unconfirmed - there's a possibility that Maja is related to Liza Marklund, a famous Swedish crime writer.

Home land

Willa

I didn't know exactly where his friend lived but I knew the estate. As I approached, something was wrong, I could feel it in my body, I broke out in a sweat as I saw Aaron. For a moment or two I was too shocked to register what I had just witnessed. He was clutching his stomach, blood seeping out from his hands, his eyes full of horror as he looked down and collapsed on the floor. I knelt down and rocked him gently back and forth, tears pouring from my eyes. I became aware of another presence. I looked up.

I'd only seen him once at the party that Emily had. He came with a group of five or six others. I recognised him because he was tall and was being a drunken idiot at the party. He looked me in the eye, still with the bloody knife in his hand. It was all happening in slow motion. After a moment's hesitation he launched at me. As he did, a piece of paper fell out of his hand. I picked it up, deftly avoiding his aim, then I ran like hell.

The gentle clang as my earring dropped to the ground. My hand went up to my bare ear. I fought the urge to turn around and pick it up. I quickened my pace as I heard shouting behind me. My heart racing. I couldn't outrun him – I had two seconds to make a decision. I made a left turn and found myself in a busy market. I saw him turn and curse when he couldn't see me. I held my breath closed my eyes and began to count, willing him to disappear. I had made myself invisible.

Mel

Obituary
89-year-old Cyril Fought, a World War Two veteran, sadly passed away in his sleep last Tuesday. He had four children, thirteen grandchildren and four great grandchildren..... yadda, yadda, yadda....

The news room was silent other than the furious tapping of keys. Deadline for the evening edition was in 30 minutes but I wasn't concentrating – I still had three other pieces to write. The wedding of Susan Johnson and Peter Briggs, two society high flyers with more money than sense. Dull as dishwater. The birth of quadruplets (cut and paste job from last year's story) and another obituary of some wealthy widow who left her 12 billion inheritance to the Cats Protection League (seriously nuts). I looked out of the floor to ceiling window to the passers by on the street below. I joined the furious tapping of keys.

Destined for Cambridge: Is a Grade A student really mixed up in postcode war?

18-year-old Aaron Coset, a grade A student from South London, was stabbed to death yesterday afternoon in Archway in what the police believe to be a gang-related incident.

"This tragic event has left me and our local community shocked and devasted. My son was a youth ambassador and a role model. He had no reason to be in North London yesterday."

The police are investigating and urge anyone who has any information to come forward. Is he really the latest victim in a postcode war or is this part of a larger crime network? A 17-year-old female was seen fleeing from the scene and police are anxious to find her so she can help with their enquiries.

Mel Wats - Post.

I pressed send. I still had ten minutes to do the other three articles. Two minutes before deadline I had them done and sent, the adrenaline had kicked in and my head was buzzing.

"Coffee?" said Ella, who sat opposite me and covered the lonely heart ads.

Ella already had her coat on and passed me mine, I grabbed my scarf, catching up with her at the lift.

Ten minutes later we were back. As the lift door opened, both of us clutching our cappucinos, shivering from the cold, I saw the new senior editor standing by his door. I nudged Ella, for he was easy on the eye.

"Want a word, Mel!" he yelled from his office, across the news room. He went back inside and closed the door. I didn't know he knew my name. The rumours were that he was ruthless and cutting.

I walked towards his office dazed bumping into several desks and spilling my cappuccino on route. I had a brown stain over my white blouse and a very sore knee by the time I got there. I stood for a moment outside his door, to knock or not to knock? I didn't knock, went straight in and launched into my spiel I had been practising.

"I'm sorry," I said before he could speak. He stood there bemused. "For what?" His eyes twinkling a little. I ploughed on, get it over with. "I know that I've been warned and that I'm an apprentice and light news stories are my remit but..." I said, gulping for air (say it, otherwise you will never say it), "if I have to cover another crocodile coming out of a toilet or another 'Hello' wedding or another eccentric old biddy dying I might crawl into a toilet and not come out."

There's always cleaning jobs I thought. Finishing completely running out of steam. Although if I did I might need to reasses my living arrangments. Maybe I could live in... I stood there expectantly. He was silent, his expression unfathomable. Please speak, please speak, willing him to fill the silence. When I could bear it no longer I began to talk again... back track... "Although I do like my job..."

He put up a hand to stop me, a smile forming on his lips. "Go investigate," he said. I let out my breath and instinctively went to hug him. I stopped myself in the nick of time... His eyes grey and sparkled.

Renetta Fake has a passion for the written word that has been with her since childhood. The invention of the internet has helped her share her written words with others. Renetta has sporadically shared her writing with friends and family but now is extending into the wider community, maybe even the world! She has not been published yet, aspirations and inspiration drive her towards it. Being a mother, a grandmother and in a professional working environment, Renetta uses every opportunity to inspire her writings.

Renetta lives and works in Waltham Forest, with her children and grandson.

Reaching home

Dear 15 year old Lorna,

You always believe you are wrong but you are not. Difference is ok and it doesn't hurt anyone. If people feel hurt by the fact you are different then you are not responsible for their feelings. You make some bad choices but you work hard and love big and somehow that makes things alright. You learn to use your mistakes to help others make better choices, even if they don't make better choices you can feel good about giving them choices by sharing your own experiences.

Nobody is perfect but you are perfectly you. There is no such thing as a perfect Mother and you can only do the best you can with the information and knowledge you have. You will learn new things and life will get brighter and YOU will have choices.

You aren't what others tell you you are, you are who you believe you are and that is ok. You don't have to fix everyone; in fact the only person you can fix is yourself. Just because others don't love you the way you wish they would it doesn't mean they don't love you at all. If people don't like you it is not a measure of yourself but it does tell you something about them, you will learn to accept and tolerate because of that.

Anger can be healthy if it is used in right action and you will learn to use it to drive yourself forward into a world of knowledge you don't yet know exists. Using your mind is attractive and although it scares some people it is not a sin to use it. In fact you will get immeasurable pleasure from doing just that and watching others learning to use their minds too.

Adults aren't as scary as they seem right now and one day you will learn that they don't actually exist. Society will tell you that you have to be one but actually it is an unreachable target, we all carry our inner child with us as we ride the rollercoaster of the years and our inner child is never far away in times of joy or pain. You will remember the playful times of your youth and will have several childhoods, never too late or too many :)

You believed that love is enough and it is! You will have a family that respects and loves and fights and argues and hugs and cares and accepts you as you are and you will make it. You will think you got it all wrong but stick with it because you got it all right, not by others standards perhaps, but by yours.

Love from 41 year old Lorna xxx

Toddler charms

Bottles strewn around cluttered room, remnants of joyful times and gloom.
Displayed against cotton wraps for cheek, fallen from skin smooth and sleek.
Rosy red face filled with youth, twinkle of ivory, newly cut tooth.
Jumping, stumbling and sounds of joy from a squidgy tumbling toddler boy.

Tiny attire swinging on heater, not time to organise, arrange or make neater
The aroma of infantile foodies, clings to soft flesh and causes no moodies.
The garments that once were white, congealed by substance, what a fright!
Tubby hands maul, grip and drop the dishes and morsels escape eager wishes.

A tender touch, a squeal of pain, bandaged then magically kissed better again.
Perfectly podgy, silky toes, where they are bound for nobody knows.
Slaps upon tiles by hands and feet, a musical melody that sounds so sweet.
Milk stained garb covering playful limbs, no wish to follow my adult whims.

Ducking, diving and hiding from what? Tissues chasing the lines of snot.
Answered by adults with curved lips who interact with meaningless quips.
Lay gently down on childish cover, no time to watch or desire to hover.
Babbling nonsense flies past grown up ears, sounds of amusement and of tears.

Fluffy rain clouds, (such scenic charm), when hair on his head lies on my arm.
Mother races in hopeful glee with no time to dream or consume cups of tea.
Velvet soft skin rests on a throbbing breast, eyelashes rested against my chest.
Rhythmic snuggles, now time to doze, cushioned softly his security he knows.

Keeping a very watchful eye and ears straining for a wakeful cry.
Folding and sorting things crushed, all movements are fast and silently hushed.
Breathing is stilled, a kiss is planted, plump arms reach, lullabies are chanted.
A tiny man stretches, he wriggles his feet, scooped up, not missing a single beat.
A moment to view the bundle so neat, love spills over, heart full, complete.
Swaddled with arms so tender and sure, a love connection untainted and pure.

Too late to read adventures in books, have a bath or wipe webs out of nooks.

Pilar Awa started to write poetry as a young person and continues doing so to this day. She started writing short stories when she moved to London, sending them in letters to her nieces and nephews in Spain. Pilar is also a singer and songwriter; in recent years she has been using song, poetry and short story as a teaching tool for her community work and political activism. In 2011 she published a DYI zine called *Myth Story of a Healing Journey* which captures her learnings in the many years long path of recovery from domestic and sexual violence. Her current work in progress is a poetry zine called *...tell me again that I can fly.*

She has been transformed and inspired by the work of writers like Maya Angelou, Starhawk, Arundhati Roy, Ursula Le Guin and Audre Lorde to name a few.

Pilar believes that words, rhythm and sound have a huge transformative power, that they can make us healthier, happier and more courageous. She believes that we need stories and poetry which show us a vision of the world we want to create and she would love to be one of those writing them in the years to come.

Our home... This broken and beautiful world

It is an ancient dance
a spiralling of Love
and betrayal
I join the motion
and open the heart to both
to the uttermost beauty
and the most painful horror
I dance & open the heart to both
to speak, to sing, to dance
what IS

War and love making
Rape and spring blossom
Pomegranates, apples, cherries…
and the horrors of famine
The faces and voices
of my nieces and nephews
then the screams
of a tortured child

A forest covered in winter snow
then a field covered in landmines
A look of recognition and love
in the eyes of a stranger
then queer bashing, race attacks,
lynchings and fascists marching

How can I see both?
open to both & remain one?

Homelessness, poverty,
Addictions, jails…
then the smell of bread,
the taste of wine,
the glow of a candle
How can I see both?
how can I open to both and
remain one?

bringing peace to the heart,
peace to the heart
Being here with you fully
Remembering both Always
Opening my feet to the
Pulsing earth
to rescue the strength,
the inner power
to keep walking the path
with wide open senses
with wide open dreams
with wide open hands
with wide open hear

Soul home

When I felt the roots of trees

entwined like a cradle under me

When I slid my hand

through a hole in the earth

and knew the water table was near

When I heard an ancient story

in the voice of a witch

When I learnt of women's loving

When I saw a fox in the twilight

and we both held our breath

When I knew I was not alone

When I travelled to the spirit world

and heard Animals talk

When we all danced naked

under the rain

When I smelled spices in your skin

When I felt one with the stars

and slept in the ocean depths

When I learnt the history of my
people

and wrote their songs

When I understood Injustice

When mother said she loved me

When I learnt stillness

When I stepped on my path

and every time I've cried

and every time I sing

Returning home after a history of displacement

No one can own the land the rivers,
the lakes, the oceans

the desert, the rocks, the mountain

No one can own another their body,
their time, their work

My people, our people for thousands
of years

have been driven away from home by
war and domination…away from
home

we are lost, uprooted, hungry

…and now is the time of returning

we are finding the routes in our
dreams like birds in flight

like the salmon in the river against
odds and strong currents

globally we return the yearning is for
belonging the compass is in our
hearts,

in the softness of surrender…and
Home is in the trees

they want to cut down,

In the lakes they want to poison

In the reefs that will die

Unless…. We…. Act….

Home is challenging white
supremacy

is in the voices of women

in Transgender voices,

Home is in giving up punishment

in dismantling the prison

growing food, reshaping gender

exposing police brutality and violence
everywhere

Home is in true safety and caring for
Each other

Our place…. in the occupied squares

with the miners' striking and the
cleaners picketing

Our place… in every corner

where resistance blossoms

the yearning is for belonging

to the darkness and the flames to the
breathing of stars

to the singing of the dawning

Graham Millington was born in Cannock just over sixty-one years ago and gained his first literary credit at twelve, after writing a small play which was performed in a school assembly. On leaving school and university, he spent time in engineering and banking, before moving to Waltham Forest to commence his mathematics teaching career.

On retirement in 2012, Graham took his writing more seriously and during the year he had a short story and poems included in an anthology and two poems performed by The Goat Theatre Company – for which he was paid the princely sum of two pounds. Graham had an article accepted by the Mathematics Association magazine and several more are pending. His interest in comedy prompted him to form a comedy writing group and its members are working hard in the hope of achieving future success. Currently Graham is writing a number of mathematics lesson plans for parents to use with their children.

Graham has aspirations to write magazine articles, a maths textbook and comedy plays. He would also like to get paid for his work but more than that, he wants his work to be read and enjoyed by others.

The second home

It had been thirty years since I first saw this street sign secured to this wall. It had told me that I had found the right place and my career was about to start. Looking down the street now, I saw the neat houses that had replaced the school. It was indeed the end of an era.

At the start of the era I had joined the school's teaching staff as a probationary teacher and was indulgently confident. I really wanted to do well and had excelled at training college. Naively I thought I was a 'star' and would set the world of maths teaching on fire. By the end of term, I was more concerned about the pupils setting me on fire.

I was awful and the sustained rejection of my efforts by many of the pupils eroded my enthusiasm and confidence. I didn't understand why they refused the life-enhancing learning I offered and why they seemed to hate me.

One colleague counselled me cynically, "Everyone loses at first but over time we learn how to lose better. Eventually we all find our way to survive."

However Brenda, a former head at the school put me straight. I had told her only half-jokingly that I had returned after Christmas only because my girlfriend made me.

"The kids can be very challenging," she smiled.

"I know," I interrupted. "Like yobs."

Brenda winced. "No, not like yobs, like damaged children."

I felt ashamed as she continued, "They act tough and hard but their defiance and rejection is just their armour. Their world is harsh, their streets paved with sewage not gold. Their parents are on the edge; many are poor and sickly. They're just stressed out, scared and confused children."

Brenda was slightly built but exuded a calm and warmth that was wholly endearing. She had been an outstanding teacher and I could see why. You paid attention to Brenda because she paid attention to you.

"You cannot get through to the kids unless you make the effort to know them as people first; test scores second," she told me. "Reach out to them, befriend them, give them your time. They need your time most of all."

So I spent hours designing engaging lessons; I didn't let them provoke me into anger regardless of their transgressions and I chatted to them; told them jokes and enquired about their day. I ran a soccer team, helped with the school play, started a games club and gradually they softened. I ran the most popular homework detention ever because I gave the miscreants biscuits and cola. "You're here to work not starve," I told them. They thought me eccentric but remarkably, I began to enjoy their company.

By Easter few pupils were problems, my superiors were amazed and I was confident again. Over the holiday my girlfriend had become my wife and although pleased with my progress, she chided me gently over the time I spent at school.

"It's your second home," she said.

Then one day during break time, I found a forgotten duffel bag in class. Searching it for the name of its owner, I found ten packets of white powder. It was Desmond's bag.

Desmond was an A-level student whose streets were paved with deeper sewage than most and yet he rose above it all to excel academically. Mum was a 'user', step-dad was in jail and it was left to Desmond to parent his three younger siblings and work after school to supplement the family income. I admired this young man for his guts and tenacity and I gave him extra tuition and the occasional bus fare. I also appreciated how school had become an oasis of calm and consistency for him. School was his 'happy place', his second home.

But as I pondered what finding the ten packets meant, Desmond returned to the classroom. "Don't panic Sir, it's not what you think..."

I said, "Good; let's go to the head and you can explain why."

"No sir, don't tell. It's Mum; we need the money for the kids". Desmond was tall and lithe and good looking and he was pleading with me. "Don't tell Sir, I won't do it again."

"Ten packets," I said. "You're a dealer."

"No Sir; they're for a friend."

I said, "You're going to need help. We'll get social services..."

But he interrupted, "He'll get the police; I'll go down. Don't tell sir, please..."

Desmond was scared and I was floundering. This was too much to deal with. I needed to get out.

I told him as calmly as I could, "Let's go to the head. It's for the best. You'll get help."

I moved to the door and for a second he seemed to square up to me. I waited.

"Please don't," he said quietly. "I'll lose everything."

After telling the head I asked, "I suppose it's a social services issue isn't it? The police won't be told?"

"I know what to do" he said, but I insisted. "There's no need for the police. It's a social work matter. He's a damaged child."

"Leave it with me," he said coldly.

Later I was called to his office and two uniformed police officers greeted me. Desmond was excluded from his 'happy place', his second home. He must have been distraught and desperate. By accident or design, within weeks he was dead having crashed a stolen motorbike into the wall near the school. He had, indeed, lost everything.

I was devastated and called Brenda to ask "Was I right in telling the head?" She put the phone down.

I changed schools and during the following years I turned my confused guilt into almost obsessive activity. I achieved a leadership role but lost my marriage in the process. School became not just my second home, but my 'preferred' home. But then with due irony, my school was 'stolen' by an Academy and I was retired. Suddenly I had no home.

So here at Desmond's wall my teaching era started and here it would finish. In between, Desmond had never been far away.

I placed flowers at the base of the wall and whispered, "We're both homeless now Desmond. I was wrong. I'm sorry."

With that, I entered my next era.